LOST OR DAMAGED LIBRARY MATERIALS

THE CARE OF LIBRARY MATERIALS IS THE <u>RESPONSIBILITY OF THE BORROWING PATRON</u>. TAX DOLLARS SHOULD NOT BE USED TO RE-PLACE OR REPAIR MATERIALS ABUSED BY INDIVIDUALS. A FEE SCHEDULE HAS BEEN SET TO REFLECT THE <u>COSTS</u> TO THE LIBRARY OF <u>REPLACING</u> OR <u>SPECIAL HANDLING</u> OF LOST AND DAMAGED MATERIALS.

MATERIALS WERE SELECTED AS AN INTEGRAL PART OF THE LIBRARY COLLECTION, AND FOR THE USE OF ALL PATRONS. IF A BOOK IS OUT OF PRINT, THE SUBJECT AREA WILL STILL NEED TO BE RESTORED DUE TO THE LOSS OF THE MATERIAL.

FEES WILL BE CHARGED AS FOLLOWS:

DAMAGE

1. <u>VISIBLE DAMAGE</u> (WATER, COFFEE, INK, ETC.) WHICH REDUCES LIFE OF MATERIAL BUT STILL CAN CIR-CULATE.....................$2.00

2. DAMAGE REQUIRING <u>ANY SPECIAL HANDLING</u> (SAND, PENCIL MARKS, ETC.).....................$3.00

3. DAMAGE REQUIRING THE BOOK BE REBOUND.....................$6.00

Loss

THE REPLACEMENT COST OF THE MATERIAL WILL BE CHARGED, PLUS A $2.00 MATERIALS AND HANDLING FEE.

IF THE MATERIAL ITSELF CANNOT BE REPLACED: 1.) THE PRICE WE PAID WILL BE CHARGED PLUS A $2.00 PROCESSING AND HANDLING FEE FOR A NEW BOOK. 2.) A FLAT FEE OF $10.00 WILL BE CHARGED TO REPLACE THE LOSS TO THE COLLECTION.
(THE AVERAGE PER-VOLUME COST OF A BOOK IS $23.00)

Selected Poems

SYLVIA TOWNSEND WARNER

Selected Poems

with an afterword by Claire Harman

VIKING

VIKING
Viking Penguin Inc.
40 West 23rd Street,
New York, New York 10010, U.S.A.

First American Edition
Published in 1985

ISBN 0-670-80850-4
Library of Congress Catalog Card Number 85-40540
(CIP data available)

Printed in England by SRP Ltd, Exeter
Set in Palatino

C 1

Contents

The Mortal Maid 9
An Afternoon Call 9
Song 10
The House Grown Silent 11
White Magic 11
The Alarum 12
The Sailor 13
The Soldier's Return 14
The Lenten Offering 14
The Rival 15
Nelly Trim 16
Epitaphs 20
East London Cemetery 21
Thaelmaon 21
"Now in this long-deferred spring . . ." 22
"Fair, do you not see . . ." 23
A Woman out of a Dream 23
Early One Morning 24
On the Eve of Saint Thomas 25
Elizabeth 26
from Opus 7 27
The Green Valley 33
Winter Moon 33
"There is a mountain's-load of trees . . ." 34
A Man in a Landscape 34
"Of the young year's disclosing days —" 36
"The vinery has been broken . . ." 37
Trees 38
"Through all the meadows . . ." 39
Song from a Masque 39
A Burning 40
"Walking through the meadows . . ." 40
Waiting at Cerbere 42
Benicasim 42
El Heroe 43
Some Make This Answer 44

Road 1940   45
The Scapegoat   46
A Song about a Lamb   46
"Some Joneses, Prices, Morgans . . ."   47
Building in Stone   47
Lines to a Cat in a London Suburb   48
Theodoric   49
Potemkin's Fancy   50
Faithful Cross   51
The Burning-Glass   52
"Mankind is always the partisan of
      Prometheus . . ."   54
Astro-Physics   55
A Journey by Night   57
Mr Gradgrind's Country   60
Thomas the Rhymer's Country   61
The Wife of King Keleos   61
Monsieur de Grignan   62
"Captain John Smith . . ."   63
King Duffus   64
Anne Donne   65
Earl Cassilis's Lady   65
Gloriana Dying   66
Wish in Spring   68
Woman's Song   68
"Fie on the heart ill-swept . . ."   69
Plum Tree from China   70
Three Poems   71
"Bubbles rise . . ."   72
Four Poems   72
Dr Johnson's Cat   73
An Acrostical Almanack, 1940   74
Awake for Love   80
"Ah, sleep, you come not . . ."   81
"I said, foreboding . . ."   82
"I thought that love . . ."   82
"Drawing you, heavy with sleep . . ."   83
"The winters have melted . . ."   83

"And past the quay . . ."   84
"Farewell, I thought . . ."   84
"How this despair enjoys me!" 85
"In a foreign country . . ."   85
"Under the sudden blue . . ." 87
In the Valley   89
"When she was young . . ."   90
"On this plain house . . ."   90
In April   91
Azrael   91
"The birds are muted . . ."   92
"How fare my ash-trees now?" 92

Afterword by Claire Harman 95

The Mortal Maid

As a fish swimming through the water's glimmer
I wooed you first,
When to the wishing well you stooped your visage
And slaked your thirst.

With a hair plundered from the white beard of Merlin
You shall be tied;
With a grass ring plighted you shall come at nightfall
To be my bride.

The straight rain falling shall be the church walls,
And you shall pace
To where an old sheep waits like a hedge-priest
In a hollow place.

In his inheritance of the kingdom of Elfin
Your son shall be born,
And you shall christen him in the dew that glistens
On the holy thorn.

An Afternoon Call

To shelter from the thunder-drench
A scorched and sorefoot tramping wench
Came to my door and proffered me
Lilac, that I had viewed her wrench
Out of my neighbour's tree.

I bade her in. With glances keen
She eyed my well-found kitchen, scene
Of kind domestic arts;
Like one who curious and serene
Looks round on foreign parts.

She talked of winds and wayside fruits,
Seas, cities, fair-times, landmarks, routes
Of journeys past and gone.
I gave her an old pair of boots
That she might wander on.

Song

She has left me, my pretty,
Like a fleeting of apple-blows
She has left her loving husband,
And who has she gone to
The Lord only knows.

She has left me, my pretty,
A needle in a shirt,
Her pink flannelette bedgown,
And a pair of pattens
Caked over with dirt.

I care not for the pattens,
Let 'em lie in the mould;
But the pretty pink bedgown
Will comfort my lumbago
When midnights are cold;

And the shirt, I will wear it,
And the needle may bide.
Let it prick, let it rankle,
Let my flesh remember
How she lay against my side!

The House Grown Silent

After he had gone the wind rose,
Buffeting the house and rumbling in the chimney,
And I thought: It will roar against him like a lion
As onward he goes.

Seven miles before him, all told —
Chilled will be the lips I kissed so warm at parting,
Kissed in vain; for he's forth in the wind, and kisses
Won't keep out the cold.

Closer should I have kissed, and fondlier prayed:
Pleasant is the room in the wakeful firelight,
And within is the bed, arrayed with peace and safety.
Would he had stayed!

White Magic

Young man, be warned by me,
  And shun the hour
  When the full moon has power
To sway men like the sea.

I with my love kept tryst
  One moonlight night.
  Something did us affright —
And she went home unkissed.

We saw as clear as day
  The thing we knew;
  Only the sky more blue
Seemed, and the grass grown grey.

Round us the orchard trees
   Like spirits stood —
   When she threw back her hood,
She looked like one of these;

So blanched the face I knew
   It seemed estranged:
   Its moonlight aspect changed
My eager blood to dew.

Disheartened, we returned;
   Nor met again.
   I have grown old since then,
But I have never learned

By what mysterious art
   The moonlight thieves
   Colour from the young leaves,
And passion from the heart.

The Alarum

With its rat's tooth the clock
Gnaws away delight.
Piece by piece, piece by piece
It will gnaw away to-night,

Till the coiled spring released
Rouses me with a hiss
To a day, to another night
Less happy than this.

And yet my own hands wound it
To keep watch while I slept;
For though they be with sorrow,
Appointments must be kept.

The Sailor

I have a young love —
A landward lass is she —
And thus she entreated:
"O tell me of the sea,
That on thy next voyage
My thoughts may follow thee."

I took her up a hill
And showed her hills green,
One after other
With valleys between:
So green and gentle, I said,
Are the waves I've seen.

I led her by the hand
Down the grassy way,
And showed her the hedgerows
That were white with may:
So white and fleeting, I said,
Is the salt sea-spray.

I bade her lean her head
Down against my side,
Rising and falling
On my breath to ride:
Thus rode the vessel, I said,
On the rocking tide.

For she so young is, and tender,
I would not have her know
What it is that I go to
When to sea I must go,
Lest she should lie awake and tremble
When the great storm-winds blow.

13

The Soldier's Return

Jump through the hedge, lass!
Run down the lane!
Here's your soldier-laddie
Come back again.

Coming over the hill
With the sunset at his back —
Never be feared, lass,
Though he look black;

Coming through the meadow
And leaping the watercourse —
Never be feared, lass,
Though his voice be hoarse;

Belike he's out of breath
With walking from the town.
He will speak better
When the sun's gone down.

The Lenten Offering

Christ, here's a thorn
More poison-fanged than any that you knew:
On the north side of the churchyard it grew,
Where lie the suicides and babes chance-born.

Christ, here are nails,
Once driven in, will never lose their hold:
Forged at Krupp's, Creusot's, Vickers', and tipped with gold
Pen-nibs that signed the treaty of Versailles.

Christ, here's a sharp
Spear, can wound deeper than all other spears:
In baths of human blood and human tears
Tempered, and whetted on the human heart.

The Rival

The farmer's wife looked out of the dairy:
She saw her husband in the yard;
She said: "A woman's lot is hard,
The chimney smokes, the churn's contrary."
    She said:
"I of all women am the most ill-starred.

"Five sons I've borne and seven daughters,
And the last of them is on my knee.
Finer children you could not see.
Twelve times I've put my neck into the halter:
    You'd think
So much might knit my husband's love to me.

"But no! Though I should serve him double
He keeps another love outdoors,
Who thieves his strength, who drains his stores,
Who haunts his mind with fret and trouble;
    I pray
God's curse might light on such expensive whores.

"I am grown old before my season,
Weather and care have worn me down;
Each year delves deeper into my frown,
I've lost my shape, and for good reason;
    But she
Yearly puts on young looks like an Easter gown.

15

"And year by year she has betrayed him
With blight and mildew, rain and drought,
Smut, scab, murrain, all the rout;
But he forgets the tricks she's played him
    When first
The fields give a good smell and the leaves put out.

"Ay, come the Spring, and the gulls keening,
Over her strumpet lap he'll ride,
Watching those wasteful fields and wide,
Where the darkened tilth will soon be greening,
    With looks
Fond and severe, as looks the groom on bride."

Nelly Trim

"Like men riding,
The mist from the sea
Drives down the valley
And baffles me."
"Enter, traveller,
Whoever you be."

By lamplight confronted
He staggered and peered;
Like a wet bramble
Was his beard.
"Sit down, stranger,
You look a-feared."

Shudders rent him
To the bone,
The wet ran off him
And speckled the stone.
"Dost bide here alone, maid?"
"Yes, alone."

As he sat down
In the chimney-nook
Over his shoulder
He cast a look,
As if the night
Were pursuing; she took

A handful of brash
To mend the fire,
He eyed her close
As the flame shot higher;
He spoke — and the cattle
Moved in the byre.

"Though you should heap
Your fire with wood,
'Twouldn't warm me,
Nor do no good,
Unless you first warm me
As a maiden should."

With looks unwavering,
With breath unstirred,
She took off her clothes
Without a word;
And stood up naked
And white as a curd.

He breathed her to him
With famished sighs,
Against her bosom
He sheltered his eyes,
And warmed his hands
Between her thighs.

Strangely assembled
In the quiet room,
Alone alight
Amidst leagues of gloom,
So brave a bride,
So sad a groom;

And strange love-traffic
Between these two;
Nor mean, nor shamefaced —
As though they'd do
Something more solemn
Than they knew:

As though by this greeting
Which chance had willed
'Twixt him so silent
And her so stilled,
Some pledge or compact
Were fulfilled.

Made for all time
In time unknown,
'Twixt man and woman
Standing alone
In mirk night
By a tall stone.

His wayfaring terrors
All cast aside,
Brave now the bridegroom
Quitted the bride;
As he came, departing —
Undenied.

But once from darkness
Turned back his sight
To where in the doorway
She held a light:
"Goodbye to you, maiden,"
"Stranger, good night."

Long time has this woman
Been bedded alone.
The house where she dwelt
Lies stone on stone:
She'd not know her ash-tree,
So warped has it grown.

But yet this story
Is told of her
As a memorial;
And some aver
She'd comfort thus any
Poor traveller.

A wanton, you say —
Yet where's the spouse,
However true
To her marriage-vows,
To whom the lot
Of the earth-born allows

More than this? —
To comfort the care
Of a stranger, bound
She knows not where,
And afraid of the dark,
As his fathers were.

Epitaphs

(i)

Here lies Melissa Mary Thorn
Together with her son, still-born;
Whose loss her husband doth lament.
He has a large estate in Kent.

(ii)

After long thirty years re-met
I, William Clarke, and I, Jeanette
His wife, lie side by side once more;
But quieter than we lay before.

(iii)

A widowed mother reared this stone
To Annott Clare, aged twenty-one.
Seven live sons have I, but she
Was dearer than them all to me.

(iv)

Here lies the body of Tom Fool,
Who died, a little boy, at school
Oft did he bleed and oft did weep,
And whimpering, now has fallen asleep.

(v)

John Bird, a labourer, lies here,
Who served the earth for sixty years
With spade and mattock, drill and plough;
But never found it kind till now.

East London Cemetery

Death keeps — an indifferent host —
this house of call,
whose sign-board wears no boast
save Beds for All.

Narrow the bed, and bare,
and none too sweet.
No need, says Death, to air
the single sheet.

Comfort, says he, with shrug,
is but degree,
and London clay a rug
like luxury,

to him who wrapped his bones
in the threadbare hood
blood wove from weft of stones
under warp of foot.

Thaelmaon

Early in the morning, late in the evening
Through this quiet valley where sheep are feeding
A man goes by and a man follows.
And all things heed them though no one sees them,
Whether they walk in clear or cloudy season,
Whether eastward or westward stretch their shadows.

He who goes first is bruised and wan-featured,
Limps with slow step as though he had been fettered,
Looks long and carefully, a grave beholder;
And he who follows is alertly footed,
And in black is ceremonially suited,
And tilts a headsman's sword over his shoulder.

After they are gone the empty valley
Fills with a long sigh, with a profound query,
As though the earth's timeless breast with its brief grasses
Stirred at some thought traversing its insentience,
Came to the brink of awakening with the question
"Will he come back again, the man who passes?"

"Now in this long-deferred spring. . ."

Now in this long-
deferred spring,
blackthorn bush by the way-
side what do you say?

Summer was a burning fever,
Winter a cold fever.
I was spared by neither.

But yet your cramped boughs
are pricked with flowers.

By rote, by rote,
these blossoms I put out.
They have not anything
to do with this spring.

They are but the badge
of an old pledge.
Farewell, and overlook
these white ashes among the black.

"Fair, do you not see. . ."

"Fair, do you not see
How love has wasted me?"
"I am blind," said she.

"Blind only that youth
Knows not to look with ruth."
"Blind, sir, in good sooth.

"Once it was not so.
My glance went to and fro,
Till I grew learned in woe.

"Blind song-larks I saw,
A rabbit in a snare's claw
That the rats did gnaw.

"Men, too I beheld
By iron engines quelled,
And a sapling felled.

"Then to the witch I sped.
Take out my eyes, I said,
Plant bright gems instead."

A Woman out of a Dream

Why have you followed me so closely
Up hill and down dale,
And why in this onset of evening have you grown
So pale and so pale?

23

Why at the water's edge do you linger
With imploring look,
And what are those words which you write with a straying finger
In the weltering brook?

Many and many are the clear streams
At which there is no slaking
One's thirst, and many the passionate espousals of dreams
Broken in the waking.

"Early one morning. . ."

Early one morning
In a morning mist
I rose up sorrowful
And went out solitary,
And met with Christ.

I knew him instantly,
For his clothes were worn;
Carpenter's gear he carried,
And between us was growing
A winter thorn.

For leaf and blossom
It had drops of dew,
For birdsong, silence —
More lovely, more innocent
Tree never grew.

"Give me," said I,
And my hands forlorn
Held out, "be it only
One of these dewdrops
Hanging on the thorn."

"Of all these dewdrops,
Hung betwixt you and me,
That must die at daybreak
I own not one of them
My own," said he.

Hearing him speak thus,
Each dewdrop shone
Enfranchised diamond;
And with sunrising
All was gone.

On the Eve of Saint Thomas

On the Eve of Saint Thomas
So innocent was the grass
Of footfall, of nightfall,
In its silver rind
That it came to my mind
How rightful to consider
Is the date of Christmas
Between the first doubter
And the first martyr.

Shove, Thomas!
Push darkness away from us.
And pull, Steven!
Haul down more light from heaven.

So solemnly the sky
Carried the moon's majesty
Through a mist of hoar-frost,
As through a transparency
Of earthly-veiled heavenly

That I thought of Our Lady
Being so far gone
That the child in her belly
Shone like the full moon.

Endure, sweet Lady,
To the end of the journey!
And yet-awhile lie patient,
O Maker omnipotent!

Elizabeth

"Elizabeth the Beloved" —
So much says the stone,
That is all with weather defaced,
With moss overgrown.

But if to husband or child,
Brother or sire, most dear
Is past deciphering;
This only is clear:

That once she was beloved,
Was Elizabeth,
And now is beloved no longer,
If it be not of Death.

from *Opus 7*

When grandees feasted have, to see the abhorred
heeltaps and damaged dainties to the board
come cringing back agrees not with their taste —
eat they will not, and yet they would not waste.
Then to the butler's or the cook's discreet
beck comes the charwoman on stealthy feet,
and in a bag receives, and bears away,
the spoiling relics of a splendid day.
Time bears (my Lord) just such a bag, and deft-
handed is he to pouch whatever's left
from bygone exploits when their glories fail.
I knew a time when Europe feasted well:
bodies were munched in thousands, vintage blood
so blithely flowed that even the dull mud
grew greedy, and ate men; and lest the gust
should flag, quick flesh no daintier taste than dust,
spirit was ransacked for whatever might
sharpen a sauce to drive on appetite.
From the mind's orient fetched all spices were —
honour, romance, magnanimous despair,
savagery, expiation, lechery,
skill, humour, spleen, fear, madness, pride, ennui. . . .
Long revel, but at last to loathing turned,
and through the after-dinner speeches yawned
those who still waked to hear them. No one claps.
Come, Time, 'tis time to bear away the scraps!
　　Time came, and bent him to the priestlike task.
Once more Love Green beheld its farmers bask
in former ruin; home-come heroes, badged
with native mud, to native soil repledged
limbs that would lose their record, ten years hence,
whether they twinged for tillage or defence.
No longer was the church on week-days warmed
that special liturgies might be performed;
war-babies, too, now lost their pristine glamour,
and were as bastards bid to hold their clamour.

So Time despatched the feast; some items still
surpassed his pouch, though; one of these, the bill.
Many, for this, the hind who pinched and numb
faced the wet dawn, and thought of army rum;
many the mother, draggled from childbed,
who wept for grocer's port and prices fled;
and village Hampdens, gathered in the tap,
forsook their themes of bawdry and mishap
to curse a government which could so fleece
on spirits under proof, and call it Peace.

    And thus it was Rebecca came to grow
sweet flowers, and only flowers. War trod her low.
Her kin all dead, alas! too soon had died;
unpensioned, unallowanced, unsupplied
with pasteboard window-boast betokening
blood-money sent from a respectful king,
she on her freehold starved, the sullen bait
of every blithe philosopher on fate.
Dig she could not. Where was the farmer who
would hire her sodden limbs when well he knew
how shapely land-girls, high-bred wenches all,
would run in breeches at his beck and call?
To beg would be in vain. What patriot purse
would to a tippler open, when its terse
clarion call the *Daily Mail* displayed:
Buckingham Palace Drinking Lemonade?
So fared she worsening on, until the chimes
clashing out peace, renewal of old times —
but bettered — sent her stumbling to the inn.
No! No reduction in the price of gin.

    A crippled Anzac saw her. "Here, I'll treat
the lady. What's your fancy? Take it neat?
Say, here's the lousy peace they talk about!"
The fire so long unfelt ran like a shout
of Alleluias all along her blood.
Reared out of her indignities she stood
weeping for joy. The soldier looked, and laughed,
and poured another, and again she quaffed,

28

and a third time. It was a rousing drink;
through weeks to come it did her good to think
it had been hers — long weeks of misery,
cold, influenza, charitable tea.
And in the spring he came once more; still lame,
not brown now, emptied of his mirth, he came,
and leaned across her gate. "Those flowers you call
wallflowers . . . I'd like a few." She gave him all.
   Mute and intent he turned them in his hand.
She watched them too, and could not understand
what charm held him thus steadfast to a thing
that just bloomed out by nature every spring.
At last he spoke, though not so much to her
as to all things around. "My great-grandfer
was bred up hereabouts; and here he courted
his girl, and married her, and was transported
for firing ricks, and left the girl behind.
He picked a young she-convict to his mind,
and settled down, and got a family.
He told my grand-dad, he my dad, him me,
all about England. When I was a pup
I felt to come to England I'd give up
all I could ever have — and here I am,
her soldier. Now, I wouldn't give a damn
for England. She's as rotten as a cheese,
her women bitches, and her men C3's.
This silly sloppy landscape — what's the use
of all this beauty and no bloody juice?
Who'd fire a rick in these days?" "Farmer Lee
fired his for the insurance once," said she.
He heard not, and spoke on. "I've come too late,
and stay too long. Ruin can fascinate
a man like staring in a cattle-hole;
that still, black water-look pulls down his soul.
England is getting hold of me. That's why
I asked you for those flowers. Good luck! Good-bye."
He turned away, and turned again, and slid
a paper in her hand. When she undid

29

its crumples she was clutching a pound note.
The liquor seemed already in her throat.

    . . .

Nature in town a captive goddess dwells;
man guards, and grilles enclose, her miracles,
the devotees who through her temples pass
with reverence keep off the new-sown grass,
and not a waft of her green kerchief, spring
down sky-forgetting bus routes signalling,
but some heart greets it, some fidelity
awaited, and with love looks back reply.
    This is her civic state. On countryside,
goddess too truly to be deified,
she a more real tribute entertains
of endless strategy, mistrust, and pains.
The farmer, slouching by his sodden shocks,
groans her a hymn, the vigilling shepherd knocks
his breast for cold, telling through every joint
a rosary of aches; hoers anoint
her floor with sweat, and the small-holder, sworn
lifelong the same sour clods to grub forlorn,
weighed with reiterated genuflexions, bows,
stiffens, warps earthward, effigy of his vows.
Them, unappeased, the immortal doxy flouts,
with floods in harvest capping seedtime droughts,
paying their toil with the derisive gold
of ragwort, tansy, and corn-marigold,
or, while their ewes breed not and their pigs die,
bidding the mole increase and multiply.
These are her common flouts; these she confers
impartially among her worshippers,
and can be borne; but hardly, when she wills
her absolute whim to manifest, and spills
foison on unlimed acres, comes a guest,
blowsily plenteous, to the harvest feast
of him whom every diligent neighbour mocks;
whose sheep stray with their scab to wholesome flocks,

30

whose dodders creep, whose seeding thistles are flown
to tended fields, and leers on him alone.
    Vainly they rail, the righteous Esau tribe —
too wise, too witless, to hold out the bribe
no woman can resist: incompetence.
Well for their peace of mind Rebecca's fence
warded sweet flowers, and only flowers, a gear
beneath their envy. With the growing year
a tide of green swept the brown earth and broke
in such a foam of colour as awoke
new being, new ambition, new delight
from the quotidian faculty of sight.
Not hers, but Nature's, was the artifice.
Do as she would, she could not do amiss
Uprooted in full bloom (and as some said
out of the churchyard furtively conveyed,
for none knew certainly whence came the trove)
pansy and gold-laced polyanthus throve.
A dead geranium from the vicarage
rubbish-heap scavenged had but to engage
root in her mould to start again to life,
and a pot lily, from the farrier's wife
cajoled, speared up though planted upside down.
    There was a Woolworth's in the market town —
the Araby, Spice Island, Walsinghame
miraculous of every village dame,
who from its many-breasted mercies drew
the joys of spending and of saving too.
Thither Rebecca went and like a child
hung o'er the tray, believing and beguiled.
Each pictured packet held a sensible hope,
lisping and sliding in its envelope —
such colours, printed bright and sleek as flames,
such flouncing shapes, and starry, and such names! —
Sweet Sultan, Arabis, Virginia Stock,
Godetia, Clarkia, Alyssum, Hollyhock,
Nasturtium, Mignonette, Canary Vine,
and Everlasting Peas, and those, more fine,

31

which bore such titles as Miss Wilkinson,
Cora, Mnemosyne, and Gonfalon.
    Returning in the carrier's motor van
she sat nid-nod, while conversation ran
blithe as a freshet over ulcered legs,
murders, spring onions, and the price of eggs.
Hesperus, the kind star which bids all home,
lightened that company jolting through the gloam,
loosened each tongue, and mellowed each fatigue;
resolving friend and foe into a league
which in that narrow heaven close-housed should dwell
in idleness like saints to hear and tell,
sitting for ever filled and never tired
in the best influence of that star attired.
Them, as though God's, the driver's countenance
out of his mirror overlooked with glance
immovable, while they whom he conveyed,
being mortal, but his hinder parts surveyed.
And like a God he, unpetitioned, knew
of each the ending and appointment due,
for each too soon arrived, when she must make
her bustle, and farewelling friends forsake.
But for those yet within, who felt the breath
of evening enter, it was but a death
that the door closed on, and the dusk estranged,
and but one hearer for more heard exchanged;
and loudlier talked the dwindling company,
and life reared up as at a funeral tea.
                    · · ·

The Green Valley

Here in the green scooped valley I walk to and fro.
In all my journeyings I have not seen
A place so tranquil, so green;
And yet I think I have seen it long ago,
The grassy slopes, and the cart-track winding, so.

O now I remember it well, now all is plain,
Why twitched my memory like a dowser's rod
At waters hidden under sod.
When I was a child they told me of Charlemagne,
Of Gan the traitor, and Roland outmarched and slain.

Weeping for Roland then, I scooped in my spirit
A scant green Roncesvalles, a holy ground,
Which here in Dorset I've found:
But finding, I knew it not. The years disinherit
Their children. The horn is blown, but I do not hear it.

Winter Moon

Tycho, a mountain in the moon
Has long ago put out his fires —
Or so astronomers avow —
And dark the crater, and cold, yet now
About my hand, about the quires
Where this night through my hand has strewn
Words unavailing, frustrate phrases,
Tycho's malignant bale-fire blazes.

A licking frost, a lambent chill,
It lights the unkindled sacrifice
And plays about me to benumb.
The words I wait for will not come,
And cowering down, as under ice
Dumb water cowers, my lost thought still
Shows me a tree upon the wold,
That stands, and cracks its heart for cold.

"There is a mountain's-load of trees . . ."

There is a mountain's-load of trees in the water.
From bank to bank the river is brimmed with trees.
Perhaps because of the smooth brushwork of the water
They do not seem to be this year's trees.

The river has no room for the shape of the mountain.
Beneath that glass runs no warrant of place or time.
It is plumed with the trees of no particular mountain
And green with a summer of no time.

This passing summer writes no word on the river
Except where a few small apples bob on the tide,
Cast off by some wilding further up the river
And carried onward by the tide.

A Man in a Landscape

Looking from where on the hill I sit
nine ricks I count,
three fields with stooks past counting,
twelve shorn pastures and two-score cattle browsing,
one barton below me, and on the skyline another,
and the shepherd's hut, bleached with winter and summer.

Narrow along the valley the road travels
with its ten telegraph poles, and out of it ravels
the stony track, mounting to the high fields of harvest
and the thistledown-cloud-scattered mute sky of mid-August.
Three hundred acres, may be, of the farm's eight hundred
lie in my sight as lies in my lap to be squandered
this hour of waiting, of willy-nilly patience;
and so I reckon up ricks and cattle, guess at the battalions
of sheaved corn, and all the landscape con and re-con.
Ah! How wearily it hangs from the shoulders of one man!

Minute on the opposite hillside, I saw him not
till the partridge brood, rousing at his slow foot,
flew up like a handful of ashes, and vanishing
designated him left alone, a labourer hoeing.
There he moiled, his fixed plover-flash of stripped-
to-shirt among the arrogant green of the turnip;
and sight brought sound with it, for now on the wind
from a mile away I heard his hoe clatter on the flint.
But at this spark of man kindled on the immense
landscape how the face of nature changed countenance,
how, at his tiny coming, the field receded, enlarged
its borders, drew away from him, and the horizon arched
its crest, developed the huge contours and implacable
of a wave about to fall.

I dare not turn my eyes from him, I dare not relinquish
that threated pinpoint of being lest it should vanish
out of the field where all day the long sun
has lit him crawling to and fro alone.
I strain my ears for the assurance that he still lives,
still turns the flints along the turnip grooves,
slow, slow . . . Ah, how slow to go,
who with each step drags after him this vast
mantle of landscape, this once-velvet now threadbare and
    trailing to waste!

"Of the young year's disclosing days"

Of the young year's disclosing days this one day —
The first of February and a Sunday —
I clasp in mind, and set down for safe keeping;
But why this one plain day more than another
Seems whimsy, unless it be that to me sleeping
You came embracing, said with your air of very
Truth: Sweet heart, this is the first of February.

Signalled thus, and thus with a kiss commended
The morning's visage looked from the blended
Duffle of winter's sober web with I know not
What of special grace, its date a portent
Pledged like the first aconite or first snowdrop,
Of its own choice and free good-will arriving
And flowered unreferred to the almanack maker's contriving.

Everything I saw — the broad sky netted over
With small white clouds like a field of clover,
The fine lace of the treetops faintly stirring
Above the boughs unmoved as though not wind plied them
But only the pressed notes of the birds conferring,
The patient winter green of the lawn, the thrushes
Hopping ungainly large under the bare bushes,

All these, that January or March might show me
Unchanged on this eastern coast, where slowly,
Hooding her bright head, planting charily
Her shreds of colour in lew of balk or hedgerow,
Muffled in guise of winter, spring comes warily,
Took, at your word's wand, the light of the spirit
In its due day incarnate, all day to wear it.

Yes, and even the sea, coiling its endless
Tether along the strand, the friendless
Unharvested one, on whose cold green ungreeted
Fall the rich rains of February Filldyke,
Looked now at peace, as though this day had meted
There too a portion of promise, as though the ambered
Forests below that green their greening remembered.

"The vinery has been broken . . ."

The vinery has been broken for years and years.
Out through the shattered panes the grape-vine rears
A green head, thrusts sideways a trailing limb.
Inside all is discarded, musty and dim.
Sheafed penny notebooks hang mouldering on the wall,
Where ten years ago someone recorded the rainfall.
Ah! — in those days the rain drummed on a sound roof.
Milky-white were the walls, the casements weatherproof,
Everything was prosperous, neat, tight and trim:
Even the weather was more orderly then than now;
And pruned was the gipsying vine, scraped every bough,
Nipped back the shadowing leaves, thinned out the bunches,
And carried into the house for dinners and lunches.
Had we come here then, had we as guests walked round
To praise the gardener, hear a host expound
August usually dry if July be wet
Our disowning going would have been sans regret.
We'd barely have liked it then, could not have loved
As at first sight we did when the vine had shoved
Its wanton garlanded head out into the opening air,
Ramping out like a cat escaping, without a care
For its weakling, undersized cluster, its one last
Derisive pledge of duteous fertility past.

37

Trees

How lovely your trees will be in winter! breathe they,
Who come this way
To warm our cold new house with belauding say;
And from this frowned-down window and that they peer,
As though in fear
Of the green ramparts standing round so solid and sheer.
Trees are always lovelier in winter, they say —
And look away,
Out-faced by that impenetrable array.

But now it is July, three months must go
Before the horns blow
And a night or two tumbles our Jericho.
Deep in the tree-tops the wood-pigeons coo,
Take two, take two!
And the trees have taken us for the whole year through.

Before the winter unarms them we must learn
The unconcern
That can walk under their towers of shade nor turn
Cold, that can tread their hundred summers beneath
Packed wreath on wreath,
And sink ankle-deep in leaf-mould nor think of death.

Best, since already they watch us and measure our pride,
Not to flinch aside,
Even at this hour when behind them their allied
Thunderstorm rears, purple cloud above green cloud,
But minute and proud
To stroll through the breathless garden with head unbowed.

"Through all the meadows . . ."

Through all the meadows they are flowing,
To all the hilltops they are climbing:
Hedgerow and hedgerow and hedgerow.
Solemn and processional and shining,
In white garments they go.

To what intention are they plighted?
Where did they wash their festal apparel
So white, and so white, and so white?
What summoned out this maymonth nonpareil?
My despair, I say, and my delight.

From my astonished heart these votive
Hawthorns have come forth in procession,
Hedgerow after hedgerow after hedgerow!
In token of my release and my ransom
In thank-offering they go.

Song from a Masque

You shall wear
Spring like a garland on your hair,
Summer like a rose behind your ear;
And the autumn wood
Shall be your riding-hood.

You shall gather
The bearded mountain to be your father,
And for your wedded love the weather;
And the inland waters
Shall dandle your sons and daughters.

But where will you go
When the north winds do blow,
When the skies are black with snow?
I pray you, begone
From us before our winter comes on!

A Burning

Blue as a forget-me-not beside the brook
flows the constant plume of the bonfire smoke,
tingeing the winter-wasted meadow where no folk
walk now, nor lovers couch under the oak,
that holds out arms bare and broke.

Blue as a forget-me-not . . . and though you are gone,
out of your field your smoke-proxy burns on,
and like a flower is living and lovely in the landscape wan,
and from dusk will gather the pallor of a swan,
and declare its red heart-beats anon.

But foul is its taint far-blown, and terrified
the cattle huddle all to the windward side.
Only I wander here, and snuff still unsatisfied
the stench of the bed they burn, the bed where you died,
the bed to me denied.

"Walking through the meadows . . ."

Walking through the meadows, to the sound of my tread
Words march through my head.
To a hundred hearts they are gone, and the hearers are won,
And march with me confident through this evening of summer
    begun,
And their thronging footsteps and mine are as one.

But a man comes here, and around me shadowless
Stretches the wide grass.
My own shadow I see and the shadow of a tree,
Million-flecked field flowers and a gull wheeling to the sea,
And the man from his work coming on to me.

Out of his day's loneliness he sights me friendly . . .
All my words are ended.
"The weather holds," say I, and he answers me, "Aye,
We are in surely for another drought. Ther's no rain in that sky
And the mid-May pasture is no more than ankle-high."

What words can I find for him, what deeds declare
That his heart will hear?
The breaking of chains will not loosen the locked rain,
And a world however new-made must cringe when winter
    comes again,
And the wind blows to men's bones the old pain.

Through his sky the sickle moves to reap but the dark,
And his heel the spark
Hammers from the senseless flint where the cart-ruts print
Unchanging over changeless slopes the curves of least dint.
What words like new-come summer can re-mint

His stoic grey to green, summon his sap forth
To change the look of earth?
What deeds his hope retrieve that he may believe
Man also on a May-day shall rouse to blossom and leaf,
And bear to autumn's barn his full sheave?

Whence the word? He it is must prompt me to it.
His trudging foot
Hammer my heart till shaped and known the plough-share
    purpose be shown,
The field cloven, the seed strewn, the handsome harvest full-
    grown.
He coming with a sickle shall reap his own.

Waiting at Cerbere

And on the hillside
That is the colour of peasant's bread,
Is the rectangular
White village of the dead.

No one stirs in those streets,
Out of those dark doorways no one comes,
At the tavern of the Black Cross
Only the cicada strums.

And below, where the headland
Strips into rock, the white mane
Of foam like a quickened breath
Rises and falls again;

And above, the road
Zigzagging tier on tier
Above the terraced vineyards,
Goes on to the frontier.

Benicasim

Here for a little we pause.
The air is heavy with sun and salt and colour.
On palm and lemon-tree, on cactus and oleander
a dust of dust and salt and pollen lies.
And the bright villas
sit in a row like perched macaws,
and rigid and immediate yonder
the mountains rise.

And it seems to me we have come
into a bright-painted landscape of Acheron.
For along the strand
in bleached cotton pyjamas, on rope-soled tread,
wander the risen-from-the-dead,
the wounded, the maimed, the halt.
Or they lay bare their hazarded flesh to the salt
air, the recaptured sun,
or bathe in the tideless sea, or sit fingering the sand.

But narrow is this place, narrow is this space
of garlanded sun and leisure and colour, of return
to life and release from living. Turn
(Turn not!) sight inland:
there, rigid as death and unforgiving, stand
the mountains — and close at hand.

El Heroe

Nobody knew his name.
Pen nor paper will tell it.

We saw him rise up singing
Where the freshet leaps and falls.
With a gun at his shoulder,
Among the briars and brambles
His blue overalls
Were like a taunt sent ringing
Out to the eyes of the rebels.

The mountain wind arising
Keened all night for woe;
Midnight laid on his face
A handkerchief of snow;

43

Dawn came with a handful
Of woodland flowers to strow;
Like mourners through the hills
The freshets began to flow.

Nobody knew his name.
Pen nor paper will tell it.

Some Make This Answer

Unfortunately, he said, I have lost my manners,
That old civil twitch of visage and the retreat
Courteous of threatened blood to heart, I cannot
Produce them now, or rig up their counterfeit.
Thrust muzzle of flesh, master, or metal, you are no longer
Terrible as an army with banners.

Admittedly on your red face or your metal proxy's
I read death, I decipher a gluttony to subdue
All that is free and fine, to savage it, knock it
About, taunt it to stupor, prison it life-through;
Moreover, I see you garnished with whips, gas-bombs,
        electric barbed wire,
And affable with church and state as with doxies.

But from other brows than yours I have felt a stronger
Voltage of death, walking among my fellow men
I have seen the free and the fine wasted with cold and
        hunger,
Diseased, maddened, death-in-life-doomed, and the ten
Thousand this death can brag have reckoned against your
        thousand.
Shoddy king of terrors, you impress me no longer.

Road 1940

Why do I carry, she said,
This child that is no child of mine?
Through the heat of the day it did nothing but fidget and whine,
Now it snuffles under the dew and the cold star-shine,
And lies across my heart heavy as lead,
Heavy as the dead.

Why did I lift it, she said,
Out of its cradle in the wheel-tracks?
On the dusty road burdens have melted like wax,
Soldiers have thrown down their rifles, misers slipped their
    packs:
Yes, and the woman who left it there has sped
With a lighter tread.

Though I should save it, she said,
What have I saved for the world's use?
If it grow to hero it will die or let loose
Death, or to hireling, nature already is too profuse
Of such, who hope and are disinherited,
Plough, and are not fed.

But since I've carried it, she said,
So far I might as well carry it still.
If we ever should come to kindness someone will
Pity me perhaps as the mother of a child so ill,
Grant me even to lie down on a bed;
Give me at least bread.

The Scapegoat

See the scapegoat, happy beast,
From every personal sin released,
And in the desert hidden apart,
Dancing with a careless heart.

"Lightly weigh the sins of others."
See him skip! "Am I my brother's
Keeper? O never, no, no, no!
Lightly come and lightly go!"

In the town from sin made free,
Righteous men hold jubilee.
In the desert all alone
The scapegoat dances on and on.

A Song about a Lamb

"O God, the Sure Defence
    Of Jacob's race,
Lover of innocence
    And a smooth face,
Accept my sacrifice —
A little lamb, bought at the market price.

"With fleece so soft and clean
    And horns not yet
A-bud, the creature's been
    The children's pet.
And sore they wept to see
Their snub-nosed friend come trotting after me."

God heard: the lightnings brake
  Forth in his honour;
But by some slight mistake
  Consumed the donor.
The lamb fell in a muse —
But soon took heart, and leaped among the pews.

"Some Joneses, Prices, Morgans . . ."

Some Joneses, Prices, Morgans, all in black
Troop to the chapel of Llangibby fach —
A parallelogram of yellow suet
That's finished off with a small vinegar cruet;

And other blackened Morgans, Joneses, Prices,
Who prefer litanies and such devices
Attend Saint Dogwell's church of the same parish —
In Rhineland Gothic, neat but somewhat garish;

And all the blackbirds into the mountain are flown
Where the wind preaches from a pulpit of stone:
A vexed doctrine, full of contention and cavil
But in such Welsh spoken as none can rival.

Building in Stone

God is still glorified —
To him the wakeful arch holds up in prayer,
Nightly dumb glass keeps vigil to declare
His East, and Eastertide;

The constant pavement lays
Its flatness for his feet, each pier acquaints
Neighbour, him housed; time-thumbed, forgotten saints
Do not forget to praise;

All parcels of the whole,
Each hidden, each revealed, each thrust and stress,
Antiphonally interlocked, confess
Him, stay, and him, control.

Whether upon the fens
Anchored, with all her canvas and all her shrouds,
Ely signal him to willows and clouds
And cattle, or whether Wren's

Unperturbed dome, above
The city roaring with mechanic throat
And climbing in layer on layer of Babel, float
Like an escaping dove,

Or whether in countryside
Stationed all humble and holy churches keep
Faith with the faith of those who lie asleep,
God is still glorified;

Since by the steadfastness
Of his most mute creation man conjures
— Man, so soon hushed — the silence which endures
To bear in mind, and bless.

Lines to a Cat in a London Suburb

Quadruped on a bough,
Cat absolute, Cat behind
All cat-shows of your kind,
I see and salute you now:

Massive, tenacious, bland,
Sardonically surefooted,
Pacing along the sooty
Aspen branch, and fanned

By all the obsequious Spring
To ear fine-furred and strong
Squat nose conveys song
Or scent wave-offering;

As pace in stealthy hope
Through incense cloud and *Tu
Es Petrus* hullabaloo
Cardinals into Pope.

But more compactly wise,
More serpentine in sin
(My more than Mazarin)
Your commerce with the skies;

While vacant and serene
Your eyes look down on me,
In all the wavering tree
The one unshaken green.

Theodoric

Praise the great Goth, Theodoric!
Who, a true patriot, led
His northern hordes into Italy,
Where he'd be better fed.

Sturgeon, peacock, assafœtida —
Nought came amiss to him
(Though Peter Vischer of Nuremberg
Makes him out to be slim.)

Only once did his appetite
Quail at a new dish;
When they served up an aged senator
In the shape of a large fish.

The dead eyes glared reproachfully —
Fear spawned in his blood
Agueish pangs innumerable
As fishes in the flood.

Not furs of marmot and zibeline,
Nor a great fire near-by,
Could warm the wretched Theodoric
As he lay waiting to die;

Chattering about old Symmachus,
And Boëthius his friend,
Who with no consolation but philosophy
Made a far braver end.

Potemkin's Fancy

I salute thee, great Catherine,
With a strange device.
See how imperiously the torches shine
Through the walls of ice!

Steep are those walls, and thick,
And glister like tears.
Each with a torch, a seven-foot candlestick,
Stand the tall grenadiers.

Icicles are not more rigid
Than these who stand to attention,
Nor heart of empress and statesman more frigid
Than this pleasure-house of my invention.

Within are the singers and trumpets,
Venice masquers and French wine,
The fairest virgins and the noblest strumpets
Of old Rurik's line,

And the English ambassador at sixes and sevens
How to sleep through such pomp:
Without is the wolfish gaze of the freezing heavens
And the frozen swamp.

Brandish your flambeaux, great Catherine!
Let all Europe admire
A palace hewn out of winter as from a mine
And streaming with fire.

But the clear walls stand fast:
They melt not, neither do we,
Inexorably bewintered in the blast
Of a measureless ennui.

Faithful Cross

Strange, that his sorrow should
Only be understood
By two rough pieces of wood.

The friends that lingered there,
However true they were,
Had grief of their own to bear.

They stood and mourned apart:
With but half a heart
For his sorrow and smart;

They mourned, and went their way
Into Heaven to be gay.
The Cross is faithful to this day.

O Tree of Life, that root
Hast not, nor hope of shoot,
Nor but this one sad fruit —

Thou, not Mary or John —
Thou, that he died upon
He chose for his eidolon.

Though he by a word or two
Or a look, men's hearts could woo
And knit, as none else could do;

Not one of the brotherhood
To whom he did good,
But two rough pieces of wood,

Hewn-off, exanimate,
Could carry and constate
His and his sorrow's weight.

The Burning-Glass

All day the sun looked down
On England; heath and town,
Cornland and woodland, mountain and champaign,
And the bright tangled skein

Of Thames, Avon, Severn, Trent —
　　Everywhere his beams went.
They lighted upon ships far out to sea,
　　And sifted every tree.

And few, and dull, were they
　　Abroad in England that day,
But looking up at the blue heavens overhead,
　　"Fine harvest weather," said.

Turning him to his rest
　　Within the patient West —
As though he kept the primal law in mind
　　To multiply his kind —

Throughout the land his rays
　　Set windows in a blaze;
But nowhere, save at Wells in Somerset,
　　Did a live Sun beget.

There, under cottage brows,
　　Glittered intact the spouse
Whose steadfast welcome the steadfast greeting could match,
　　And fired a neighbour's thatch.

Strange chance! (Enough to undo
　　Man's wit, might he look through
Seeing, and know the Sun an enormous spark
　　In caves of endless dark;

And, like ourselves, condemned
　　His little light to expend
By rote. But our imaginations deck
　　The heaven's hideous black.)

53

Strange chance! meeting well-met!
Chance more wild-faring yet
I woo, that with long hope and true intent
My burning-glass present

To that unmeasured, un-
surmisable incendiary of suns —
Life — that some beam of it, matched by my art,
May fire a stranger's heart.

"Mankind is always the partisan of Prometheus"

Mankind is always the partisan of Prometheus.
The God's bird, and even the God himself
Are by mere justice and victory disgraced.
Yet was the bird punctual, patient, obedient,
And the God, God. Why is it unforgivable
To be with all humility in the right?
Whence came this radiance gilding the downward
Pinions of Lucifer, and on the rebel's
Countenance this beauty of unholiness?
Oh no, not only the genius of Aeschylus!
Rather, man's heart having lost original grace
Becomes a hostel to all lost causes, cares not —
So they be lost — whether of good or evil.

Yet was the bird punctual, patient, obedient. . .

Twice I have dreamed, and twice I have been an eagle.
Happy was the first dream
For I was a brass eagle in the church.
My static wings quivered beneath the Word,
My feet were planted in a cluster of lilies,

The organ played, and the school-children sang.
Vast was the word of God, but I sustained it.
I was forever meek, strong and durable,
and shone like gold before the congregation.

But in my second dream I was the bird of Zeus.
The air breasted my breast, surged through my wings,
Bubbled and seethed about me, and streamed on,
While far beneath the range of Caucasus
Lay small and clean as pebbles in a brook
With here an agate-vein of a crevasse
And here a forest like a water-weed.
I had no care, no animus, I poised
Calm as my shadow floating on the abyss
Set like a seal upon the writ of God.
So in an endless morning I was poised,
So on a blameless errand I was aimed,
So was the bird punctual, patient, obedient.

Astro-Physics

i

As a poor clerk sums up, exact to pence,
A king's expenditure, nor wonders where,
Why, when, on whom disbursed, so he may fare
Unblamed down column and trudge homeward thence,
Astronomers compute with diligence
The spilth of light, check pulse of shaken air,
Audit the stars, this wealth with that compare,
But not this wealth with their own indigence.

Tied in its fivefold fetter, the duped mind
Amasses zeros, studies to detail
The enrichment of its lack; then unrepined

Turns back to drum the puny sensual scale,
Deaf to the ruby's steadfast note, and blind
To all the colours of the nightingale.

ii

Nought, nought, nought, nought . . . O wise Arabian!
Who, cyphering first, the primal zero wrought —
Thyself commemorating in thy nought,
Imposed on time an absence for a man.
Circling around the dust thy finger ran,
And delved the sign with such enlargement fraught
That henceforth humankind beholds all thought,
All speculation, captive in its span.

Tagged to the sum of knowledge is this terse
Nought, nought, nought, nought; is, in its quiddity,
The hollow vocative O! that cries through verse;
An O ends God; and man's brief scrutiny,
From the round world rounding the universe,
Plots out its arc upon infinity.

iii

To no believable blue I turn my eyes,
Blinded with sapphire, watchet, gentian,
Shadow on snow, Mediterranean,
Midsummer or midwinter-moonlight skies.
Unstained by light, unravished by surmise,
And uttering into the void her ban,
Her boast, her being — *I know not a man!*
Out of all thought the virgin colour flies.

After her, soul! Have in unhaving, peace,
Let thy lacklight lighten upon thee, read
So well thy sentence that it spells release.
Explore thy chain, importune suns to cede
News of thy dark — joyed with thy doom's increase,
And only by distinction of fetters freed.

I heard them say, Henceforth few stars, or none,
Shall whirl to being in galactic space.
The heavens are waxed old, and the embrace
Spent that begot the kindred of the sun.
Time quits his youth. The giants one by one
Husband the prodigal light that streamed apace
From squandered atoms, and the stellar race
More soberly to their extinction run.

Annihilation noosed them, and with fell
Contraction teaches prudence, but relents
Never, nor can, nor ever they rebel
Against self-waste until, grizzled insolvents,
They barter death for petrifaction, dwell
Onward but as his trophies and monuments.

A Journey by Night

"In this last evening of our light, what do you carry,
Dark-coloured angels, to the cemetery?"
"It is the Cross we bury.

"Now therefore while the last dews fall,
The birds lay by their song and the air grows chill
Follow us to the burial.

"It was at this hour that God walked discouraged
Seeing his olive-grove with a new knowledge
While man hid from his visage;

"It was at this hour the dove returned;
It was at this hour the holy women mourned
Over the body in clean linen wound.

"So God in man lay down, and man at long
Last in the sepulchre was reclining
And the dove laid her head under her wing;

"Only the poor Cross was left standing.

"Scarecrow of the reaped world, it remained uncarried and
          unwon;
With no companion
But its warping shadow it endured on,

"Till in this final dusk even that shadow,
Stealthy and slow, stealthy and slow
Faded and withdrew.

"So was the last desolation accomplished
And the Cross gave up the ghost.
Look on it now, look your last;

"See how harmless it lies, now it is down;
A shape of timber which in a tree began
And not much taller than the height of a man."

It lay there, naked on the bier. It was black
With tears, blood, martyrdoms, with jewels decked,
And rubbed smooth with wearing on a child's neck.

Shouldering their burden, the angels went onward,
Like a wreath of mist moving unhindered,
And like a mourner I followed.

Time was no barrier to us, for time was no more;
The tideless sea lay muted along the shore,
The city clocks registered no hour,

The last echo had ebbed from the church bells;
Silent were the barracks, silent the brothels
And the water slept in the wells.

Rivers we forded and mountain-ranges crossed;
Silent were the reeds in the marshes we traversed;
Silent as they we came to a coast

And smelled the sea beneath us and walked dry-footed
On air — gentle it was as a bird's plumage —
And a shooting-

Star went by us on its errand elsewhere.
I knew neither astonishment nor fear
Till land glimmered below me, and an austere

Sea-board of turf, shaggy as a wolf's pelt,
Bruised my being as I grounded with a jolt
On the prison-floor pavement

Of earth-bound man. The angels went smoothly on
Through a wilderness where each successive horizon
Was another sand-dune.

Time held out no promise, for time was no more.
Bones and bleached tree-roots lay scattered everywhere;
The dusk waited in vain for a star.

Suddenly the Cross scrambled off the bier.

Shouting like a bridegroom it bounded
On its one foot towards a pit dug in the sand —
A dark hole like a wound.

Poised on the edge of the pit, it began to sing.
"Lulla-lulla-lullaby" it sang. "I am home again."
And leaped in.

I saw the sand close over the pit and the suspended grey
Dusk convert to darkness in the twinkling of an eye.
"Now wake," said the angel, "and go your way."

Mr Gradgrind's Country

There was a dining-room, there was a drawing-room,
There was a billiard-room, there was a morning-room,
There were bedrooms for guests and bedrooms for sons
    and daughters,
In attic and basement there were ample servants' quarters,
There was a modern bathroom, a strong-room, and a con-
    servatory.
In the days of England's glory.

There were Turkish carpets, there were Axminster carpets,
There were oil paintings of Vesuvius and family portraits,
There were mirrors, ottomans, wash-hand-stands and
    tantaluses,
There were port, sherry, claret, liqueur, and champagne
    glasses,
There was a solid brass gong, a grand piano, antlers,
    decanters, and a gentlemen's lavatory,
In the days of England's glory.

There was marqueterie and there was mahogany,
There was a cast of the Dying Gladiator in his agony,
There was the 'Encyclopaedia Britannica' in a revolving
    bookcase,
There were finger-bowls, asparagus-tongs, and inlets of
    real lace:
They stood in their own grounds and were called Chats-
    worth, Elgin, or Tobermory,
In the days of England's glory.

But now these substantial gentlemen's establishments
Are like a perspective of disused elephants,
And the current Rajahs of industry flash past their wide
    frontages
Far, far away to the latest things in labour-saving cottages,
Where with Russell lupins, jade ash-trays, some Sealyham
    terriers, and a migratory
Cook they continue the story.

Thomas the Rhymer's Country

Time in its douce predestinating way
Manifests called and reprobate together.
Cacrahead and the Catrail were always grassed,
Craig Hill was always heather;
And there has always been the sheep on the one
And on the other the adder.

Clear as the word of God the March Burn
Runs between them. There I would paddle and ponder
Through the secure solitude of a child's afternoon
Were the choice set me whether
I would choose the velvet composure of the one
Or the besotting honey scent of the other.

Being predestined to grow up indifferent
To free-will, scarcely my own right hand neither
The right hand of God distinguishing from its left,
Now I would ask no better
Than on Craig or Cacra let fall, so there to lie
For ever and for ever.

The Wife of King Keleos

Never was such a servant.
Nothing was too much for her to do,
She could card and spin, bake and brew,
She could watch untired the whole night through,
She was modest, prudent, observant,
She knew unfailingly where all lost things were,
She was abundant as a Lammas Fair . . .
Everything throve while she was there.

Everything but my heart:
She troubled my dreaming and my waking hours,
She dulled my embroideries and sapped my flowers,
The babe upon her knee was no longer ours.
But for all her deity and her art
She could not inveigle a mother's wit;
Before I stole to the hearth and saw her sit
Dipping the child in fire I was sure of it.

Trust no gods, I say.
I have had one in my house, I should know:
Here are my crooked hands to show
How narrowly and with what piercing woe
I rescued the child. But to this day
My mind misgives me, and must, till I spread
The bridal blankets, and with the maidenhead
The last tincture of deity is shed.

Monsieur de Grignan

There are too many doves!
Forever, forever arriving, their wings have cloven
My olive screens and my grooved cypresses;
Forever alighting, they lay on my roof a burden of whiteness,
A burden of softness,
Their alighting weighs on my roof like a burden of snow.

Roo-cooing, roo-cooing . . .
I have no chamber that is not filled with their clamour;
With strut and flutter they oust me hither and thither,
Their wings bewilder my blazon, and darken my forefathers,
My coffers are stuffed up with their cast feathers;
Among them I have mislaid the man that I am.

Into my wife's lap they are flown.
Bosom and wrist and shoulders, she is doves all over
And looks at me with strange eyes through a trellis of wings.
She does not heed me, for I am becoming already
What time will make me:
A letterback cypher, the man of her mother's daughter,
The man who unloosed the doves, and remembered for that
    alone.

"Captain John Smith . . ."

Captain John Smith, that wayfaring, seafaring, lovefaring man,
Sighted a profiled headland, that glimmering through the murky
Sad sea-mist recalled a lady he'd loved in Turkey.
Mapping the coast, he mementoed his fair Circassian.
Later advices from home re-named Cape Tragabigzanda, Cape
    Ann.

There is this much in a name that a high-minded Puritan —
Anxious John Winthrop, for instance — might have thought
    twice ere he ventured
Himself, frail vessel of virtue, into a land thus indentured
To Venus by evocation of a trousered Courtezan;
But there can be no wantonness between Cape Cod and Cape
    Ann.

How oddly, too, might have developed the Republican
Party under the spell of that relaxing nomenclature,
Sages and astronomers endorsed for the Presidential Candidature
By senators lolling with Hafiz on the silken divan:
The scions of Tragabigzanda, not the stern sons of Ann.

Tragabigzanda Tragabigzanda
Foiled is the travelled amorist, recalling his Amanda,
Lost, lost to New England is Cape Tragabigzanda.

63

King Duffus

When all the witches were haled to the stake and burned;
When their least ashes were swept up and drowned,
King Duffus opened his eyes and looked round.

For half a year they had trussed him in their spell:
Parching, scorching, roaring, he was blackened as a coal.
Now he wept like a freshet in April.

Tears ran like quicksilver through his rocky beard.
Why have you wakened me, he said, with a clattering sword?
Why have you snatched me back from the green yard?

There I sat feasting under the cool linden shade;
The beer in the silver cup was ever renewed,
I was at peace there, I was well-bestowed:

My crown lay lightly on my brow as a clot of foam,
My wide mantle was yellow as the flower of the broom,
Hale and holy I was in mind and in limb.

I sat among poets and among philosophers,
Carving fat bacon for the mother of Christ;
Sometimes we sang, sometimes we conversed.

Why did you summon me back from the midst of that meal
To a vexed kingdom and a smoky hall?
Could I not stay at least until dewfall?

Anne Donne

I lay in in London;
And round my bed my live children were crying,
And round my bed my dead children were singing.
As my blood left me it set the clappers swinging:
Tolling, jarring, jowling, all the bells of London
Were ringing as I lay dying —
John Donne, Anne Donne, Undone!

Ill-done, well-done, all done.
All fearing done, all striving and all hoping,
All weanings, watchings, done; all reckonings whether
Of debts, of moons, summed; all hither and thither
Sucked in the one ebb. Then, on my bed in London,
I heard him call me, reproaching:
Undone, Anne Donne, Undone!

Not done, not yet done!
Wearily I rose up at his bidding.
The sweat still on my face, my hair dishevelled,
Over the bells and the tolling seas I travelled,
Carrying my dead child, so lost, so light a burden,
To Paris, where he sat reading
And showed him my ill news. That done,
Went back, lived on in London.

Earl Cassilis's Lady

Meeting her on the heath at the day's end,
After the one look and the one sigh, he said,
Did a spine prick you from the goosefeather bed?
Were the rings too heavy on your hand?
Were you unhappy, that you had to go?
No.

Was it the music called you down the stair,
Or the hot ginger that they gave you then?
Was it for pleasure that you followed them
Putting off your slippers at the door
To dance barefoot and blood-foot in the snow?
No.

What then? What glamoured you? No glamour at all;
Only that I remembered I was young
And had to put myself into a song.
How could time bear witness that I was tall,
Silken, and made for love, if I did not so?
I do not know.

Gloriana Dying

None shall gainsay me. I will lie on the floor.
Hitherto from horseback, throne, balcony,
I have looked down upon your looking up.
Those sands are run. Now I reverse the glass
And bid henceforth your homage downward, falling
Obedient and unheeded as leaves in autumn
To quilt the wakeful study I must make
Examining my kingdom from below.
How tall my people are! Like a race of trees
They sway, sigh, nod heads, rustle above me,
And their attentive eyes are distant as starshine.
I have still cherished the handsome and well-made:
No queen has better masts within her forests
Growing, nor prouder and more restive minds
Scabbarded in the loyalty of subjects;
No virgin has had better worship than I.
No, no! Leave me alone, woman! I will not
Be put into a bed. Do you suppose
That I who've ridden through all weathers, danced

Under a treasury's weight of jewels, sat
Myself to stone through sermons and addresses,
Shall come to harm by sleeping on a floor?
Not that I sleep. A bed were good enough
If that were in my mind. But I am here
For a deep study and contemplation,
And as Persephone, and the red vixen,
Go underground to sharpen their wits,
I have left my dais to learn a new policy
Through watching of your feet, and as the Indian
Lays all his listening body along the earth
I lie in wait for the reverberation
Of things to come and dangers threatening.
Is that the Bishop praying? Let him pray on.
If his knees tire his faith can cushion them.
How the poor man grieves Heaven with news of me!
Deposuit superbos. But no hand
Other than my own has put me down —
Not feebleness enforced on brain or limb,
Not fear, misgiving, fantasy, age, palsy,
Has felled me. I lie here by my own will,
And by the curiosity of a queen.
I dare say there is not in all England
One who lies closer to the ground than I.
Not the traitor in the condemned hold
Whose few straws edge away from under his weight
Of ironed fatality; not the shepherd
Huddled for cold under the hawthorn bush,
Nor the long dreaming country lad who lies
Scorching his book before the dying brand.

Wish in Spring

To-day I wish that I were a tree,
And not myself,
Confronting spring with a neat little row of poems
Like cups and saucers on a shelf.

For then I should have poems innumerable,
One kissing the other;
Authentic, perfect in shape and lovely variety,
And all of the same tireless green colour.

No one would think it unnatural
Or question my right;
All day I would wave them above the heads of the people,
And sing them to myself all night.

But as I am only a woman
And not a tree,
With piteous human care I have made this poem,
And set it now on the shelf with the rest to be.

Woman's Song

Kind kettle on my hearth
Whisper to avert God's wrath,
Scoured table, pray for me.
Jam and pickle and conserve,
Cloistered summers, named and numbered,
Me from going bad preserve;
Pray for me.

Wrung dishclout on the line
Sweeten to those nostrils fine,
Patched apron, pray for me.
Calm linen in the press,
Far-reaped meadows, ranged and fellowed,
Clothe the hour of my distress;
Pray for me.

True water from the tap
Overflow the mind's mishap,
Brown tea-pot, pray for me.
Glass and clome and porcelain,
Earth arisen to flower a kitchen,
Shine away my shades ingrain;
Pray for me.

All things wonted, fleeting, fixed,
Stand me and myself betwixt,
Sister my mortality.
By your transience still renewed,
But more meek than mine and speechless,
In eternity's solitude,
Pray for me.

"Fie on the heart ill-swept . . ."

Fie on the heart ill-swept
Where sorrows over-kept
Sodden with tears and foul
Lie mouldering cheek by jowl
With mildewed revenges
Grown tasteless with time's changes,
Limp wraths and mumbled visions,
Fly-blown into derisions,
Delights jellied to slime
And tag-ends of rhyme.

Life! Grant me a harder
Housewifery in my larder,
And if I may not eat
Fresh-killed meat,
Crisp joy and dewy loathing,
Let me have done with loving.
Aye, though philosophy's
Wan pulse my palate freeze
Ere I to carrion swerve
Carrion-like, let me starve.

Plum Tree from China

In the narrow garden,
Where I lay in the sun
Looking towards London,
A plum tree from China grew.

A few stammering blossoms
It put out in spring:
An idle hour's reckoning
Could have told all its leaves.

But with autumn emerging
The uncomforted tree
Reprinted unchangingly
Its Chinese Alas! upon air.

Once, and once only,
Where canker had rent
Its black bole, transparent
Oozings of amber came.

Jewels of frozen honey,
Distillation of crass
Sweet plum-flesh to topaz —
I bit and tasted one.

To this day I remember
How my dashed sense
Admitted with prescience
The taste of sterilised grief.

This phoenix-fruit long-guarded
Of the tree in distress
Had not even the bitterness
To tincture its flat wanhope.

O child well-warned, know passion
From passion's pure doll!
Dread that dewy alcohol
Of tears sublimed past salt!

Three Poems

i

Experimentally poking the enormous
Frame of the universe
This much we know:
It has a pulse like us.

But if it lags for woe,
Quickens for fever
Or calm euphoria measures it for ever
Other astronomers must show.

Learning to walk, the child totters between embraces;
Admiring voices confirm its tentative syllables.
In the day of unlearning speech, mislaying balance,
We make our way to the grave delighting nobody.

iii

Fish come solid out of the sea,
Each with its due weight of destiny.
The purposed sprat knows what it would be at,
The skate, twirling in its death agony,
Is the embodied wave that flopped down
On the fisherman's coble and left him to drown.

"Bubbles rise . . ."

Bubbles rise from the water and are domes,
Admiration burnishes them, Time tarnishes.
On a fine morning they seem to be there for ever.
Venice! Do you remember Byzantium?

Four Poems

i

Become as little children,
Said the Recruiting Sergeant;
With every hope as frantic,
With every fear as urgent.
Be seen and not heard
While the cannon volley
And sleep when you are bid
By Death, your tall Nannie.

ii

Five sons I have begot to part
In anxious feud the goods I leave.
My neighbour made a work of art
Which will not toil and cannot thieve.

iii

The infant's hand is raised in wrath,
The infant's face is red with lust,
The infant devastates the hearth —
And didst Thou make it of the dust?

iv

The Sleeping Beauty woke:
The spit began to turn,
The woodmen cleared the brake,
The gardener mowed the lawn.
Woe's me! And must one kiss
Revoke the silent house, the birdsong wilderness?

Dr Johnson's Cat

When the house has cleaned itself at last
Of its diurnal human,
When the black man and the blind woman
Both have groped their way into the dark
And the dwindling watchman has gone by,
I have heard him waken, and sigh.

I have heard the bedstead twang and creak,
And the bed-curtains swaying,
And he sprawled down on his knees, praying:
O Jesu pie, salvum me fac!
Whether that same Jesu heard him or no,
My ears attended to his woe.

An Acrostical Almanack, 1940

Virtue had a lovely face
Till a mirror showed it to her;
Now she brandishes the glass
In the face of every wooer;
And he sees a haggard elf
Scolding him, holding out to him
A cold copy of himself.

* * *

Alacoque, Alacoque,
Rumpled her maiden smock:
Thinking of the Sacred Heart
She would quiver and smart,
Each drop of its blood
Fell on her with a thud,
Pierced her like a dart.

Alacoque, Alacoque,
Swarmed up the Petrine Rock:
Not clash of keys nor frown
Under the triple crown,
Not syrup, nor scoff
Could keep the girl off,
Could keep the girl down.

Alacoque, Alacoque,
Now in a stony smock
Quietly you kneel
In the side aisle.
Under alabaster wimple
That no heartbeat can rumple
How does victory feel?

* * *

Lavender, who will buy
My sweet scented lavender? —
That ripened in July
And took so long to dry.
Oh smell it, it is sweet
Sewn in its winding-sheet
As though it did itself remember.

* * *

Envy to the counting-house
Ran, and pulled the Banker's sleeve.
Dreamy Banker, don't you grieve
These small deposits are not yours?

Do you think me poor? the Banker said.

Am I one of those whose round
Brings them here on market-day
Paying in with anxious joy
Penny as endeared as pound?

Oh, I am undone! the Banker said.

* * *

Necessity, Necessity,
Drives her wild caravan
Wherever she pleases.
Fences nor leases,
Uncles or nieces,
Edict nor prayer,
Monk nor man,
Nothing can stay her!

Onward she drives her
Piebald stallion
Over hedges and ditches,
Cricket pitches,
Kings in their riches,
And the charcoal-burner:
On, on, on!
Nothing can turn her.

Paying no licences,
Speaking only romany,
No hand has ever
Crossed hers with silver,
Though futures she'll cypher
In every paw:
Gipsy Necessity
Who knows no law.

* * *

Timon, who had
A fig-tree in his garden growing,
Walked out at the cock-crowing
And found an Athenian lad
Had hanged himself thereon, and so was dead.

And as one fruit
Duly after another ripens
Old men, boys, and maidens
Took the same leafy route
To death from Timon's tree, grief driving them to it.

Timon at last
Sent heralds crying through the city
His fig-tree would shortly
Be felled, so as their host
He begged those who'd make use of it make haste.

Too late, too late,
O Timon, to recall the sally
That proved you not wholly
Impeccable in hate
Of man, thus to man's grief compassionate.

* * *

Innocence lived on the heath,
Cracking stolen nuts with her white teeth:
Cast off by her virtuous kin
At Holy Christmas she got drunk on gin.

Innocence was no kitten:
Her memory went back to Troy and Eden;
But she was clean and hale,
With an eye like a falcon's and a tongue like a flail.

Then came a lawyer, who said:
Madam, you are no more disinherited.
England has need of you.
Old Habeas Corpus is dead, so make no ado.

He pulled off her coarse cleiding,
He dressed her all in white like a whore at a wedding;
In her cheek he drove a dimple,
And starved her till she was as small as Shirley Temple.

Now to the rich man's door
She drudges brazen-faced to beg for the poor:
She who *Arms for Spain!*
Shouted, now lisps coaxingly: *Aid for Britain*.

* * *

Naiad, whose sliding lips were mine
No longer than the nightingale
Paused between one song and another,
Where sit you now the willows throws
Her last gold to the sullen river?

Do you among your sisters tell
Yet of a kiss so weighed with woe,
So mute, so cold, you doubt the giver
Still walks about the wintry earth,
But in some deep pool drowned soon after?

* * *

Esther came to the court
Of the Eternal.
Her good deeds followed her
Like menservants and maidservants;
The tears of her children
Sparkled on her like emeralds,
The sighs of her husband
Billowed out her garments.

When Esther beheld
In the sackcloth of a widow
With a sword across her knee
Judith of Bethuliah,
She cast off her ornaments,
She bowed herself low,
Down to the foot that had arched
Over the blood of the tyrant.

* * *

Trumpeter of midday,
With a rickety grace
You step out to play
Above the market-place:
And in the clock-face
The minute hand slips free —
Tan-tan-taree!
The hour hand sets off on another chase.

Trumpeter of midnight,
With a clanking pace
You step out to affright
The echoing market-place:
And in the clock-face
The minute-hand slips free —
Memento mori:
The hour hand sets off on another chase.

Quia pulvis est —
Tan-tan-taray!
Magister adest
Et vocat te.
And over the clock-face
That's gilded broad as day
The cloud shadows play,
Catching and clearing in an endless chase.

* * *

Industry, your flax is spun,
Your linen loomed,
Your sheets hemmed,
Your washing sweetens in the sun.

Industry, your house is swept,
Your table scrubbed,
Your mirrors rubbed,
And all the while your Angel slept.

79

For while you did what should be done,
He wrote no word
Of your good deeds,
But like a white cat lay curled up in the sun.

* * *

Broceliande, dans ton hault forest
Gist Merlin le Graunt ki etoit Fay.

There he lies, hearing the wind blow;
Like grey moss his beard prickles the snow.

There he lies wrapped in a furred cloak;
His hands are tangled in the roots of an oak.

The squirrels drop down acorns on his head;
He lies there quietly, pretending to be dead!

The swineherd and the old forester
Sit by his grave to eat their provender:

He hears them talking of the fate of England;
He lies there, holding the oak root in his hand.

Broceliande, dans ton hault forest
Gist Merlin le Graunt ki moult est Fay.

Awake for Love

They are all gone to bed;
But I for love of them am still awake,
Companioning the fire that falls a-drowse;
My spirit walks around the darkened house,
And feels the wind, and sees the heavens shake
Their diamond tresses overhead.

Love has extended it
Into the changing stature of a cloud;
My arms embrace the eaves, my bosom pressed
To the cold slates yearns warm above their rest,
Over their roof-tree my vast love is bowed,
As bowed before their hearth I sit.

My wakefulness includes
Their sleep, my compact kept with time and space
Vouches for them enfranchised, their dreams glide
Unchallenged through my being, as the tide
Of guarded life-blood on with even pace
Flows through the body's solitudes.

"Ah, sleep, you come not . . ."

Ah, Sleep, you come not, and I do not chide you.
You the ever-young, the sleek and the supple,
How should I bride you
Who am so harsh with care, so grimed with trouble?

You to the child's cot and the lover's pillow,
You to the careless creation in field and steading,
And to my roof-mate swallow
Come with goodwill, who come not to my dull bidding.

Like lies down with like. If I am to woo you
I must disguise myself, and in youth's green
Habit pursue you,
Or imagine myself to what I never have been:

Or you in pity put on death's leaden likeness
To follow my weariness.

"I said, foreboding . . ."

I said, foreboding,
How shall my autumn furnish forth your spring?
How from my smouldered green,
And slaked, shall you replenish and preen?

But you, bestowing
On my dust your sun, take wing;
And risen with you, my care
Aims surer your flight, being heavier than air.

Oh then, thanksgiving
Take from this ground that you have taught to sing.

"I thought that love . . ."

I thought that love would leap from a cloud
To devour me,
Or with the loud
Unmaking challenge to be of a trumpet
Overpower me.
But love has befallen me like a sleep.

And calm as a weed I range in this flood
Where no will is.
My anxious blood
Forgets its scarlet and lies down in slumber
With the lilies,
And my thoughts for the change of clouds I exchange.

"Drawing you, heavy with sleep . . ."

Drawing you, heavy with sleep to lie closer,
Staying your poppy head upon my shoulder,
It was as though I pulled the glide
Of a full river to my side.

Heavy with sleep and with sleep pliable
You rolled at a touch towards me. Your arm fell
Across me as a river throws
An arm of flood across meadows.

And as the careless water its mirroring sanction
Grants to him at the river's brim long stationed,
Long drowned in thought, that yet he lives
Since in that mirroring tide he moves,

Your body lying by mine to mine responded:
Your hair stirred on my mouth, my image was dandled
Deep in your sleep that flowed unstained
On from the image entertained.

"The winters have melted . . ."

The winters have melted with their snows and gone.
Along the mossy walk
By the edge of the wood you beckoned me on
To hear the wooing cock pheasant talk
To his silent hen
On a young evening in May.
There I stood, leaning against you, listening —
I have never been away!

"And past the quay . . ."

And past the quay the river flowing;
And I not knowing
In what gay ripple, ambling and sidling,
The tears you wept for me go by me.

And in the ripples the bridge flaking;
Making and unmaking
Its grey parapet, and I not knowing
How in your mind I am coming and going.

And to my heart the wise river
Murmuring, Oh, never
Under the same bridge of any river
Does the wave flow twice over.

"Farewell, I thought . . ."

Farewell, I thought. How many sonnets have
Begun or ended on these syllables.
Sooner or later chimes that seventh wave
Like a ground bell among a chime of bells.
Above that steadfast note the changes veer,
And through them their begetting ending clangs:
Some time, but never, *never. Next year. This year.*
Then on the air the rigid echo hangs;
And through it one looks round and sees the sky,
The trees, the houses where men live, the small
Mounds of the dead, and live men going by,
And everything is there, and that is all.
Only the echo cries the music's over.
So it is to have loved and lost the lover.

"How this despair enjoys me!"

How this despair enjoys me! How much more throughly
Than your love could, your faithlessness burns through me!
Now, only now, you have possessed me truly.

No more in joy's inadequate day I languish.
To this last dark my last light I extinguish,
And all my being to loss of you relinquish.

"In a foreign country . . ."

In a foreign country travellers who come to stay
But not to settle, after the first day
Or two of floating buy with pleasure sophisticate
Something regional, a hat of grass or a fur hat —
A dated seizin, an acclimatisation to borrow,
Wear for a while and cast away;
But I in a strange continent bought a sorrow,
And wore it for a half-year's stay.

Being more tractable a texture than grass or fur
As time went by my sorrow became embroidered
With roads and trees, quilted with mountains, dyed
With the colours of sumach and Joe-Pye-weed.
The hulking hillsides, shaggy with hemlock and pine
And rambling like bears along the horizon,
Were my sorrow's hem:
When I walked they wallowed after me, when I swam
They swam with me, their treetop stir
Silenced in the tepid lake-water.
The rocky pasture, echoing under my footfall,
Affirmed how weighty the garment I must trail,
The fox-grape and the sweetfern chafed by the midday

85

Sun, and the accomplished perfection of decay
That evening from the alembic forest distilled
Were the odours shaken out as my sorrow rustled
From one day to another day,
And my heels in desolate idleness tapping the road
In permanence of granite were shod.

Sometimes as a breast-pin I wore a poplar tree,
And in its boughs a cat-bird complained,
And in its shade my friends sat reasoning with me.
At other times I let a river twist
Itself into a bracelet round my wrist:
Thus sweetly (saying) might a neck be noosed
In a crystal halter,
Thus streamingly salvation come by water
And all your cares be at an end.
But breast-pin I pulled out and bracelet I let fall.
There would be other trees and other rivers,
And southward a heavier mantle I trailed
Into a poor land.
There was my sorrow embroidered with patched pastures,
With a scorched hillside sagging like a drained breast,
With the ghostly regiment of the felled forest,
With the gaunt water-course, with the forsaken avenue
Beseeching the witless mansion, with the tattered advertisement
Of the snuff that wards off the fever and dulls the ague.
There through the counterfeit rose-acres
I groped onward after the cotton pickers,
Hauling my sorrow after me like a gunny-sack;
There idle and desolate amid idleness and desolation
My heels dinting the red sand or the white sand
With the silence of negation were answered back.

Sorrow in one's own country is something familiar.
Wear it or tear it, it is a homespun wear:
It is the bus route and the grocer's doorway and the scent
Of the March dust under the April rain.
It is unbought, casual, climatic, dateless, an inherited garment,

86

The shawl one's mother and one's grandmother wore,
Easy to put on and easy to mislay:
Now I can scarcely believe that I wore and called my own
Anything so magnificent
As the sorrow I bought in a strange continent
And wore for every day.

In mid-Atlantic foundered the island of Atlantis.
There toll the bronze bells of the city of Ys.
There driftingly dance upon the unvexed tides
Drowned sailors with their Atlantidean brides
(But the head being heaviest they dance heels uppermost).
And there, midway between one coast and the other coast,
Dimming, submerging, falling from the light of day,
Past colour sombred and past texture sodden,
Wallowing downward towards the lost, the foundered, the
      forgotten,
Down, down to the innocence of legend it recedes —
My sorrow, embossed with mountains, darkened with forests,
      laced
With summer lightning, quilted with rivers and dirt roads —
My sorrow, stately as a cope, vast as a basilica —
My sorrow, embroidered all over with America,
That at a word from you in mid-Atlantic I threw away.

"Under the sudden blue . . ."

Under the sudden blue, under the embrace
of the relenting air, under the restored shadow
of the bird flying over the sunny meadow,
the garden ground
preserves an unconvinced and sullen face;
as though
it yet remembered the smite of frost, the wound of snow.

87

Automatically and without grace
it puts forth monosyllables of green,
answers Yes, or No,
with a muddy daisy, or one celandine,
or in ravel of last year's weeds lies winter-wound.
Poor cadet earth, so clumsy and so slow,
how, labouring with clods, can she keep pace
with Air, the firstborn element, tossing clouds to and fro?

And yet she answers with a spurt
of crocus, and makes light
of snow with snowdrops, and her celandine
is burnished to reflect the sun.

How like your absence and this winter have been!
Long vapours stretched between
me and your light, I saw you bright
beyond them, but your shine
fondled a field not mine.

There was the illumination and there the flight
of shadows black as night;
but I looked round
ever on the same november clear-obscure of dun
and grey and sallow and ash-colour and sere;
even my snows were white
not long, and melted into dirt.
Put out your hand. Feel me. Though the spring is here
I am still cold.

Because of this, because of the winter's hurt,
because I am of the earth element,
dusky, stubborn, retentive, slow to take hold, slow to loose
    hold,
because even to my hair's ends I carry the scent
of peat and of wood-smoke and of leaf-mould,
and because I have been
so long your tillage, so deeply your well-worked ground,

you must be patient;
forgiving my lack of green, my lack of grace,
my stammering blossoms one by one
shoved out, and my face doubtful under the sudden blue, under
      the embrace
of the relenting, of the returning sun.

In the Valley

On this first evening of April
Things look wintry still:
Not a leaf on the tree,
Not a cloud in the sky,
Only a young moon high above the clear green west
And a few stars by and by.

Yet Spring inhabits round like a spirit.
I am sure of it
By the swoon on the sense,
By the dazzle on the eye,
By the long, long sigh that traverses my breast
And yet no reason why.

O lovely Quiet, am I never to be blest?
Time, even now you haste.
Between the lamb's bleat and the ewe's reply
A star has come into the sky.

"When she was young . . ."

When she was young she sang all day.
I told her she was like a wren,
So small the case, so ardent the voice.
Wait till my dying day, she'd say,
And then, then,
You'll hear me singing like a swan.

After midsummer birds fall silent
Or lose their tune, but she not so.
Still I could trace her by her voice
Through house and ground. But in the end
Like a swallow
Twittering softly she did go.

"On this plain house . . ."

On this plain house where I
Dwell and shall doubtless die
As did my plain forefathers in time past
I see the willow's light-limbed shadow cast.

I watch in solitude
Its flying attitude
Laid on that brick and mortar soberness
Like the sharp imprint of a fleeting kiss.

Just so, I think, your shade,
Alien and clear, was laid
Briefly on this plain heart which now plods on
In this plain house where progeny is none.

In April

I am come to the threshold of a spring
Where there will be nothing
To stand between me and the smite
Of the martin's scooping flight,
Between me and the halloo
Of the first cuckoo.
"As you hear the first cuckoo,
So you will be all summer through."
This year I shall hear it naked and alone;
And lengthening days and strengthening sun will show
Me my solitary shadow,
My cypressed shadow — but no,
My Love, I was not alone; in my mind I was talking with you
When I heard the first cuckoo,
And gentle as thistledown his call was blown.

Azrael

Who chooses the music, turns the page,
Waters the geraniums on the window-ledge?
Who proxies my hand,
Puts on the mourning-ring in lieu of the diamond?

Who winds the trudging clock, who tears
Flimsy the empty date off calendars?
Who widow-hoods my senses
Lest they should meet the morning's cheat defenceless?

Who valets me at nightfall, undresses me of another day,
Puts it tidily and finally away?
And lets in darkness
To befriend my eyelids like an illusory caress?

I called him Sorrow when first he came,
But Sorrow is too narrow a name;
And though he has attended me all this long while
Habit will not do. Habit is servile.

He, inaudible, governs my days, impalpable,
Impels my hither and thither. I am his to command,
My times are in his hand.
Once in a dream I called him Azrael.

"The birds are muted . . ."

The birds are muted in the bosom of midsummer.
The wind has hidden itself under her green shawl.
There it nestles and lies slumbering:
She pulls her woods over all.

O breast, too deep in peace for song or sighing,
Lean over me in the solemn sycamore bough;
Shelter me from the echoes of an old crying,
Enfold me in here and now.

"How fare my ash-trees now?"

How fare my ash-trees now?
Do my fruit-trees bear?
The gnarled apple and the stately pear —
How do they grow, and I not there, not there?

Neither more nor less
Than when you walked below.
Apple and pear tree fruit, and ash-trees grow,
And the ripe fruit falls, and leaves begin to snow.

Yes, I remember well
The plunge of apple and pear,
The whirled whisper of ash-leaves flocking down air —
But is it all as when I was there, was there?

Yes and no.
Nettles and weeds grow tall
Muffle each fruit fall:
Unsought-for lie apple and pear, and rot one and all.

Afterword

It has been a pleasure to edit this volume, choosing from Sylvia Townsend Warner's books of poetry and from a large quantity of posthumously published verse a selection which illustrates the richness and variety of her talent. Readers of her *Collected Poems* were surprised by the diversity of her skills; satire, narrative, love poem, lyric, burlesque, she can turn a hand to them all, and all of them are represented in this selection. Few poets can spread their net so wide and make such a varied yet excellent catch.

Sylvia Townsend Warner rather surprised herself by continuing to write poems all her adult life, "usually just when I'm about to pack or catch a train or have someone to stay. Always at inconvenient moments like that." Her poems are her most personal statements and have their occasions in real places and situations as much as in imagined ones. The poems cast light, therefore, not only on her life but on her fiction too. In them we become aware of the acute, almost painful significance certain places, buildings, gardens had for her; we see the vexed, sometimes virulent effects of her radical politics and sense the solemn passion of her life's love. In others there are palpable links with her novel- and story-writing, her interest in narrative and character, the speaking voice, the dramatic incident. The novelist's and poet's skills combine in some of her most immediately striking verse, in for instance "Monsieur de Grignan", "Anne Donne", "King Duffus", "Mr Gradgrind's Country" and "Captain John Smith". These poems are complete, thrifty, drawing on and pondering over the preoccupations of a wise and active mind.

The poems in this book were written over a fifty-year span, from the beginnings of Sylvia Townsend Warner's writing career in the 1920s to her death in 1978, and they are arranged in a loosely thematic, not a chronological order. The easy fluency of her writing, the sheer joy she took in doing it, are apparent here as throughout all her work. Sylvia Townsend Warner has, as she foresaw, turned out to be a posthumous poet, but whether her books wander in or out of print is rather beside the point. No fashion can extinguish writing as fine as hers.

Claire Harman